How do I use

Key Words with Peter ~~and Jane~~ parallel series, each conta~~ining~~ series are written using the same carefully controlled vocabulary. Readers will get the most out of **Key Words** with Peter and Jane when they follow the books in the pattern 1a, 1b, 1c; 2a, 2b, 2c and so on.

• Series a
gradually introduces and repeats new words.

• Series b
provides further practice of these same words, but in a different context and with different illustrations.

• Series c
uses familiar words to teach **phonics** in a methodical way, enabling children to read increasingly difficult words. It also provides a link to writing.

Published by Ladybird Books Ltd
A Penguin Company
Penguin Books Ltd., 80 Strand, London WC2R 0RL, UK
Penguin Books Australia Ltd., Camberwell, Victoria, Australia
Penguin Group (NZ) 67 Apollo Drive, Rosedale, North Shore 0632, New Zealand

1 3 5 7 9 10 8 6 4 2

ISBN: 978-1-40930-127-1

Printed in China

Key Words

with Peter and Jane

7b Fun and games

written by W. Murray
illustrated by J.H. Wingfield

Peter and Jane are on holiday at the home of their aunty and uncle. They are not going out this morning because it is wet.

"What do you want to do this morning?" Jane asks Peter.

At first Peter says that he does not know. Then he says, "I know, let's make a kite, like the one I saw in a book."

He gets the book for Jane. "There," he says. "Look at this. It's not like the kite we had from the shop. Will you help me to make it?"

Jane looks in the book. "It tells us how to make it here," she says. "There are pictures of it. Yes, I'll help you, it will be fun. Let's make it now."

The brother and sister get the things they want for the kite.

Peter says," We can fly the kite on the sands when the rain stops."

They see their aunty as they make their kite. Peter tells her that they are going to make a kite.

"Why do you want to make another one?" Aunty asks.

Peter says, "It'll be fun to make it, and it won't be like our other kite."

"We'll have one for Peter and one for me," says Jane.

Jane helps Peter to make the kite. Now and then they look at the pictures in the book.

"Let's make it red," says Peter.

"No," says Jane, "let's make it blue."

"We'll make it blue and red," says Peter.

Soon the nice new kite is blue and red. Aunty comes in to see it.

"It's a very nice kite," she says. "I hope it will fly."

Jane looks out of the window. "We will see if it'll fly this afternoon," she says. "The sun is out again."

It is the afternoon, and the sun is out. The two children go down to the sands with their new kite. They keep away from the other boys and girls and from the donkeys, so that they can run along the sands.

"We must not get in the way of the donkeys," says Jane.

Peter says that Jane can have the kite first. "You can pull it first," he says.

Jane runs along with the kite. She makes it go up, but then it comes down. She has another go and then gives the kite to Peter.

Peter runs very fast with the kite. Soon it is going up and up. Peter stops, but the kite keeps on going up.

"Just look at that," calls out Jane.

"It's going up like a bird," says Peter.

Some other children look up at the kite. They talk to Peter and Jane about their nice new kite.

Peter and Jane have a happy time on their holiday, away at the sea. Here they are at play on the sands. Aunty and Uncle are not with them this afternoon.

The two children run along the sands to fly their kite. First Peter has the kite and then Jane has a go with it. The brother and the sister let some of the other children play with them.

Then Peter lets the kite go out of his hand.

"Look," calls Jane. "It's going out to sea."

Peter says, "The kite is not going up any more. It will come down now. It will come down in the sea."

"We'll make another one," says Jane.

"No," says Peter, "we may get this one back. We have a friend who could get our kite out of the sea for us. Let's go to find our friend to tell him about this."

The friend of Peter and Jane is Jack, a big boy who knows their aunty and uncle very well. Jack has a motor boat. The two children look for him for some time.

Then they find Jack in a café on the pier. He is with his friend.

Peter and Jane tell Jack that their kite is in the sea. They ask him to help them to get it out of the water.

"Please take us out in your motor boat," they say. "Then we can get our kite."

Jack tells Peter and Jane that he will help them to get their kite back.

They come out of the café and go to the motor boat. It is a big boat. Peter and Jane have been in it before. They all get in, and then Jack makes the boat go.

"I hope that we bring the kite back," says Jane.

"So do I," says Peter.

The sun is on the water as they go along in the motor boat. Jack makes the boat go round the end of the pier and then out to sea.

Peter and Jane like it in the motor boat. "I like your boat very much," says Peter to Jack. "I wish we had a boat like this."

The boat can go very fast, but Jack does not make it go fast today. He can see many children by the sea, and he looks out for any who may be in the water.

"Where did your kite go?" he asks.

They tell him where they think it is. As they go along they all look in the water for the kite.

Then Peter says, "I think I can see it. Look over there. Look over there by that other boat."

They all look, and soon they see the red and blue kite in the water.

"Go on, Jack," says Peter. "Make the boat go up to the kite. I'll get it out of the water."

"No," says Jack, "you keep your seat. I'll get it. I don't want you to go into the water. We don't want that. What would your mother and father say if you did?"

He makes his boat go on and then brings it round by the kite.

"Keep your seats," he says again to the children.

Peter and Jane keep in their seats as Jack stops the boat. Then he puts his hand into the water and gets the kite. He pulls it into the boat and looks at it.

"It's a nice kite," he says.

Jack gives the kite to the children. They are happy to have it back.

"Thank you, Jack," says Jane. "It was good of you to help us find our kite. We can play with it again now."

Soon the boat is going along. Peter lets the kite go up and he pulls it along after the boat.

"Don't let go again," says Jane.

"We must go back now," says Jack.

"What's the time?" asks Peter.

"It will soon be five o'clock," says Jack.

"Do you think we would have time to have an ice-cream in the café on the pier?" Peter asks Jane.

"No," says Jane, "there's no time for an ice-cream. It'll soon be five o'clock. We always have tea at five o'clock. We should not get home in time if we had an ice-cream in the café."

The motor boat comes to the pier. Jack's friend is there. "So you found your kite," he says to the children.

Peter says, "Yes, we found it, thanks to Jack."

Jack and his friend go into the café on the pier and the two children go off home.

Aunty says to Jane, "I am going to make some ice-cream this afternoon. Would you like to help me, dear?"

"Yes, please," says Jane. "I should like that very much. I always like to help you."

"May I help?" asks Peter.

"Yes, dear, why not?" says Aunty. "Boys as well as girls like ice-cream."

Aunty gets the things they want and she talks to the two children as she makes the ice-cream.

"I know how to do it now," says Jane. "I think I could make some."

"So do I," says Peter. "You and I will make some when we get home."

As the three of them sit down to eat the ice-cream, the dog comes in to see them.

"He likes ice-cream," says Aunty.

"Yes, he wants some now," says Peter.

"Can we give him some?" asks Jane.

When Aunty says she can, Jane gives the dog a little of her ice-cream.

The children can see their uncle from the window as he gets out of his car.

They always like to see him when he comes home, but today they want to see him very much. He has been to the shop to buy a present for them.

"He said he would buy our present today," says Jane. "Can you see if he has it with him, Peter?"

"I think so," says Peter, "and I think I know what it is. He is going to bring us a Punch and Judy."

Just then Uncle comes in the door. The two children run up to him.

"Well, Uncle?" says Jane. "Did you go to the toy shop today?"

"Yes," says Uncle. "I've been to buy your present. I hope you like it. It's Punch and Judy."

"We love Punch and Judy," says Jane. "Do let us see them."

"Here you are, then," says Uncle.

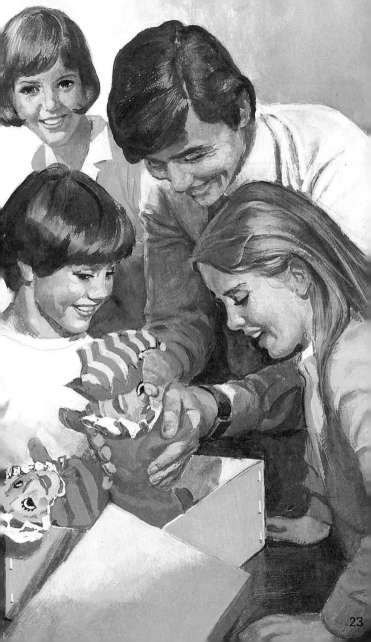

Uncle says, "You put Punch and Judy on your hands, like this. Then you make them talk."

"I see," says Peter. "I know the right way to do it now. Let me have Punch, I like him very much."

Peter puts Punch on one of his hands.

Then Jane says, "I'll have Judy. I know the right way now." She puts Judy on her hand. "I like Judy," she says.

Peter makes Punch say, "I'm Punch. I would like to live here with Peter."

Jane makes Judy say, "I'm Judy. I like Jane. I like this house."

Then Punch and Judy talk to one another. The two children have fun.

"I would like to take them to school to let the other children and our teacher see them," says Peter.

"Yes," says Jane, "let's take Punch and Judy to school when we go back."

They thank Uncle for his present.

There has been some rain, but now it is a hot day. The children know their holiday will soon come to an end, so they want to go on the sands again.

Uncle and Aunty say they will take them down to the sands. "All four of us will have a picnic tea," says Aunty. Peter and Jane like that.

When they get down to the sands they all go into the water. Then they play with a ball for some time. After that Uncle says it is too hot for him. He puts on his hat.

Peter and Jane sit by their uncle and play with the sand. They talk as they play.

"I wish the hot sun would come out every day," says Jane.

"Yes, I'd like to go in the sea and play with the sand every day," says Peter.

As they play they put sand on their uncle for fun.

The two children are to go home today. Their mother has come to take them back on the bus. She is with Aunty now. Mother and Aunty have much to talk about.

"All good things come to an end," says Peter. "We've had a good time here with Aunty and Uncle, but it will be nice to see Bob and Mary Green again."

"Yes, I want to see them and Molly and Pam," says Jane.

"What about Grandmother and Grandfather?" asks Peter. "We want to see them as well."

The two children have Punch and Judy on their hands. "We'll have some fun with Punch and Judy," Jane says.

Aunty calls them. "Come on, Peter and Jane. It's time to go."

Peter and Jane go to Aunty and Mother.

"We want to thank you and Uncle very much for our holiday," Jane says to Aunty. "We love to be in your home."

The two children are back at their own home. They are very happy to be with their mother and father and all their friends again.

Jane writes a letter to send to her aunty and uncle. In it she thanks them again for the holiday. Peter writes a letter to their old friend Tom who lives by the sea. Mother helps them to write the letters.

After this the brother and sister go out to send off the letters. They take the dog Pat and Jane's doll Ann for a little walk.

Then they go into the house next door to see Mr and Mrs Green and Bob, Mary and Molly.

They have much to talk about. They want to know how their friends are and where they have been. Then they tell them about their holiday.

They all look at the kite and Punch and Judy. Jane tells her friends she can make ice-cream.

Peter and Jane go for a picnic. They walk for some way in the woods and find a nice place they know. They have their tea there. The sun is out but it is not hot in the woods.

When they have had tea the two children go on into the woods. They think there is a road in the woods which will take them to the farm.

After some time Peter says to Jane, "I don't know the way to go. We have never been here before. Do you know the way?"

"No," says Jane, "there are too many trees for me to see the way. I don't know where we are."

"I know what to do," says Peter. "I'll get up a tree. I think I could see the way from up there."

"Don't get into danger," says Jane, as she helps Peter up the tree. He says there will be no danger.

Peter is in the tree. It is a big tree. Jane looks up at Peter as he gets to the top.

"I like it up here, Jane," he calls. "It's fun."

"Can you see the road?" asks Jane.

"Yes," says Peter, "I can see the road. I can see the way we have to go to get to the farm."

"Can you see the farm?" asks Jane.

"Yes," says Peter, "I can see the farm, and I can see a fire. There's a fire by the farm, Jane."

Peter comes down from the tree.

"Come on, Jane," he says. "I know the way now." They go on.

Soon they see a woman out for a walk with her dog. Jane asks her if she knows the way to the road.

"Yes," says the woman, "the road is over there."

"Does the road go to the farm?" asks Peter.

"Yes, it does," says the woman.

The children thank the woman and go on to find the road. They go along the road and then come out of the wood.

Soon they can see the farm.

"There it is," says Jane. "There's the farm."

"Yes," says Peter, "you can see the fire now. I hope the farm is not on fire."

They go on to the farm. They find that the farm house is not on fire, but that the fire is next to it.

The men from the farm are there. Peter and Jane look on as some of the men put water on the fire. Others look after the horses.

The horses do not like the fire, and the men take them away from it to another place.

Pam comes to talk to Peter and Jane. She tells them about the fire

"It looks like rain now," says Peter. "If it rains it'll help to put out the fire."

The men put out the fire with water, and the rain helps them.

Then Peter and Jane walk home in the rain. Pam's father does not take them to their home in his car because of the fire. He has to be at the farm with his men and the horses.

The two children get very wet in the rain as they go home, but they think it is fun.

A van comes along the road. In it is a man they know very well. He says he will take them home.

"Get in the van," he says. "Come in out of the wet, Peter and Jane. I'll take you home."

The brother and sister talk to him as they go along. They tell him about the fire at the farm.

The van soon gets to the road where the children live. They thank the man for his help and go into their home.

Peter and Jane are back at school. They like their school and their teacher. The teacher gets some of the children to talk to the others about their holidays.

One boy talks about his holiday on the sea. He was with his mother and father on a motor boat. They were very happy, he says. It was a big boat and he and his Dad liked to fish from it.

One of the girls tells about her holiday on her grandfather's farm. There were cows, pigs and horses on the farm and she liked to help with them.

Peter talks about his own holiday by the sea with his aunty and uncle. He tells about the fun they had on the sands and about the kite.

Jane tells the others about Punch and Judy and the donkeys on the sands.

Then all the children make pictures of the things they did on their holidays. They write about the pictures.

The teacher tells the children she wants all of them to make one very big picture. They will all work on the one picture. Every boy and girl will do some of it.

"What's this big picture to be about?" asks one boy.

"We'll call this big picture 'Our Day'," says the teacher. She writes 'Our Day' for the children to see and read.

Then she says, "In the picture you can put all the things you do, from the time you get up to the time you go to bed."

The teacher tells the children to think about the picture and to talk to one another about it.

They talk about all the things children like, about sweets, ice-cream, cakes and apples and other things to eat. They talk about balls, dolls, kites and other toys. They talk about games, shops and money, and about cats, dogs, rabbits, horses, donkeys, birds and fish.

Here are the children at work on the big picture. In the first girl's picture you can see a girl in bed. It is the morning and it is time to get up. The sun looks in at the window.

In the next picture a boy and a girl eat with their mother and father before they go to school.

The teacher walks by the big picture. In it she can see boys and girls going off to school. Then there are children in school at work. After this some boys and girls are out at play. They play games with other children and with their toys.

One girl talks to the teacher about her picture. "This is my garden. Here are some birds," she says.

The boy next to her says, "This is me in the picture. Mum gave me some money for some eggs and I'm going to the shop for them."

In Jane's picture you can see Jane and Peter with their mother and father at a picnic. "It's too hot in the sun," she says, "so we're in the woods."

There are many trees. Jane draws Peter in the picture. "The trees are just right for him," she says. "He likes to get up to the top of a tree."

"Here's a dear little rabbit," she says. "It has found something to eat. It doesn't see the dog."

Another girl comes up to talk to Jane about her picture. "Why doesn't the dog run after the rabbit?" she asks.

"The dog cannot see the rabbit," Jane says, "and I wouldn't let my dog have the rabbit."

"I like your picture," says Jane's friend. "Have you any more to do to it?"

"Yes," says Jane, "I'm going to put some birds in it now."

"I wish I could live by the sea," says Peter, as he works on his picture. "I should like that."

You can see the blue sea and the sands in Peter's picture. There are boats on the water and some children on the sands. The sun is out and the children are at play.

Another boy looks at Peter's picture and talks to him about it. "They all look happy in your picture," he says

"Yes," says Peter, "they are all on holiday, and it's hot. There are many things for the boys and girls to do."

He puts in some donkeys, with some children on them.

"Now for Punch and Judy," he says. "All boys and girls like Punch and Judy."

"What about the motor boat?" asks his friend.

"I'm just going to put the motor boat in," says Peter. "Here it is. I'll put my friend Jack in it. It's going out to sea."

Mother is in the garden as the children come home from school. She loves to work in her garden.

"I put you in a picture today," says Jane to her mother. She tells her about their day at school.

Then Mother sends Peter and Jane with some money to the shops to get some things for her. Peter and Jane like to help their mother.

"I'll get the tea now," says Mother as they go. "You can have it when you come back."

The children soon come back from the shops. As they have their tea they talk some more about the big picture at school. "Our teacher thinks it's very good. She's going to keep it so that Mothers and Fathers can see it when they come up to the school," says Peter.

"I think it must be a very nice picture," says Mother. "Dad and I would like to see it."

New words used in this book

Total number of new words: 68
Average repetition per word: 12